KU-029-520

Contents

Chapter 1: The big project 5

Chapter 2: All tried out 13

Chapter 3: The perfect portrait ... 19

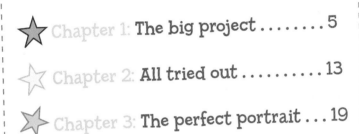

Chapter 1
The big project

It was time for art, which was Zoe's favourite lesson. Today Zoe saw a giant canvas hanging in the front of the art room.

"What is that thing?" Max asked.

"It is the giant canvas for our self-portrait project! We are finally doing it!" cried Zoe.

"You've been waiting all year for this project," said Max.

Every year, the Year 2 class painted a giant canvas. It was hung in the library.

"For the next two weeks, you'll practise on paper. Then you'll paint your portrait onto the canvas," said Mr Baker, their art teacher.

Mr Baker drew an oval on the board. With two lines, he divided it into four equal parts.

"Okay," he said. "Let's get our proportions right. Eyes go on this line. The nose goes here."

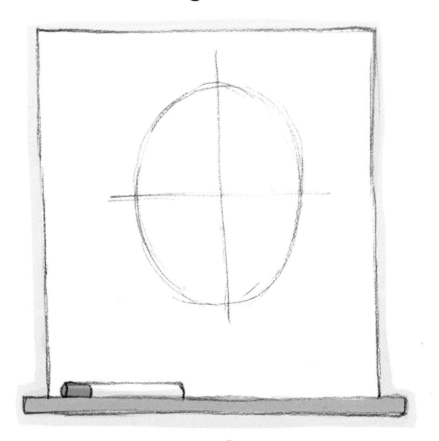

Max listened and watched. Zoe didn't listen or watch. She quickly drew her self-portrait.

"It's not a race, Zoe," whispered Max.

"Mr Baker always shows my art
as the best example," she said. "So
I have to get it done first."

Mr Baker finished talking. Zoe
ran over and showed him her
drawing.

"I've finished. You can show it to everyone," she said.

"Hmm," he said. "Where should the eyes be?"

Zoe frowned.

"I think you need to start again," Mr Baker said.

Then Mr Baker held up Max's drawing.

"Look, everyone," he said. "This is a great example of proportion. Good work, Max!"

Zoe threw her drawing in the bin.

The next week, Zoe studied

Mr Baker's portrait examples.

She studied her face in a mirror

too. Then she began to draw.

"This looks stupid," she said.

"No it doesn't! Keep going,"
said Max.

Zoe tried her best, but it was
hard. She tried drawing her eyes.

"These don't look right,"
she said.

Max tried to block the bin. But

Zoe threw her drawing in anyway.

Max said, "You'll get it, Zoe."

So she tried again.

"My ears don't belong there," she groaned.

Zoe tore the paper into pieces and threw them on to the table.

"I don't like art any more,"

she said.

"Don't say that," said Max.

"Keep trying."

"I'm all tried out," said Zoe.

The bell rang and the art lesson was over. Max could draw a perfect self-portrait. Zoe couldn't even draw a nose!

Zoe put her head down on her desk and sighed.

That night, Zoe felt better. She called Max.

"Please come over," she said.

"I need your help."

"I'm on my way," Max said.

Zoe and Max spent every night that week drawing.

Max drew Zoe. Zoe drew Max. Then they worked on drawing their own faces.

Every night, Zoe got better.

Max was a good teacher.

"I think I like art again," Zoe said.

"What a relief!" said Max.

The next day, Mr Baker said they would go in alphabetical order to paint. That meant Zoe was last.

When Mr Baker finally called out Zoe's name, she was ready.

Zoe hurried to the canvas and studied her square. Then she grabbed a brush and painted her self-portrait.

She took her time and did her best.

"Done," she said and grinned. "That's me, all right!"

"It sure is," said Mr Baker.

"And it's a perfect portrait," said Max.

"I agree," said Zoe.

About the author

Shelley Swanson Sateren is the award-winning author of many children's books. She has worked as a children's book editor and in a children's bookshop. Today, as well as writing, Shelley works with primary-school-aged children in various settings. She lives in Minnesota, USA, with her husband and two sons.

About the illustrator

Mary Sullivan has been drawing and writing all her life, which has mostly been spent in Texas, USA. She earned a BFA from the University of Texas in Studio Art.

Glossary

canvas thick, strong cloth used to paint on

divide to separate into parts

feature any of the different parts of the face

portrait a picture of a person

proportion correct size or place of something compared with other things

self-portrait a picture of yourself made by yourself

Discussion questions

1. Zoe was excited about her art project. Talk about something that you are excited about in your favourite lesson.

2. Why is it important to watch and listen to your teacher?

3. At the end of the story, Zoe is proud of herself. Talk about a time when you felt proud of yourself.

Writing prompts

1. Look in a mirror and study your face's features. List three shapes that you see.

2. What is a skill that you worked hard to learn? Write a few sentences about that skill.

3. What is the best project you ever did in art? Write down your answer and your reason.

Make your own portrait

The hardest part of drawing portraits is getting the proportions right. You can practise with these fun steps.

What you need:

- 1 unlined A4 sheet of paper
- pencil with rubber
- 1 bowl, about 12 cm wide
- ruler
- crayons, felt tips, or coloured pencils

What you do:

1. Put the bowl upside-down in the middle of the paper. Draw round it to make a circle.

2. Using the ruler edge, draw two crossing lines that divide the circle into four equal parts (see page 8). Draw a small dot where the lines meet.

3. Draw the eyes on the centre line. The inside of each eye should be about 2 cm from the centre dot.

4. Draw the top of the nose at the centre dot. The bottom of the nose should be halfway to the chin. Make the bottom of the nose as wide as the inside of the eyes.

5. Draw the mouth halfway between the chin and the bottom of the nose. Make the mouth as wide as the centre of the eyes.

6. Draw the top of the ears at the centre line. The bottom of the ears should line up with the bottom of the nose.

7. Rub out the lines. Add hair, then colour your portrait.

The fun doesn't stop here!

We have lots more Max and Zoe adventures for you to enjoy!

Discover more books
and favourite
characters at
www.raintree.co.uk